Hero Dad

by **Melinda Hardin**
illustrated by **Bryan Langdo**

two lions

two lions

Amazon Publishing, Attn: Amazon Children's Publishing, P.O. Box 400818,
Las Vegas, NV 89140
www.amazon.com/amazonchildrenspublishing

The illustrations are rendered in Winsor and Newton watercolors and
F pencils on Farbriano Artistico extra white, cold pressed watercolor paper.
Book design by Vera Soki   Editor: Marilyn Brigham

Printed in Mexico
5 6 4

Library of Congress Cataloging-in-Publication Data

Hardin, Melinda.
 Hero dad / Melinda Hardin ; [illustrations by] Bryan Langdo. — 1st ed.
    p. cm.
 Summary: A child demonstrates that while Dad differs from a traditional
superhero, as an American soldier he is a superhero of a different kind.
 ISBN 978-0-7614-5713-8
 [1. Superheroes—Fiction. 2. Soldiers—Fiction. 3. Father and child—Fiction.]
 I. Langdo, Bryan, ill. II. Title.
 PZ7.H21772Her 2010
 [E]—dc22
                                        2009029343

Dedicated to the children at Grafenwoehr Elementary, Grafenwoehr, Germany
    —M.H.

For Grandpa Langdo
    —B.L.

My dad is a superhero.

He doesn't wear rocket-propelled boots—
he wears Army boots.

He can't fly—
well, sometimes he can.

He doesn't have X-ray vision—
he has night vision.

He doesn't drive a super-powered car—
he drives a tank.

He doesn't wear a cloak that makes him invisible— he wears camouflage.

He doesn't carry a laser gun—
he carries a rifle.

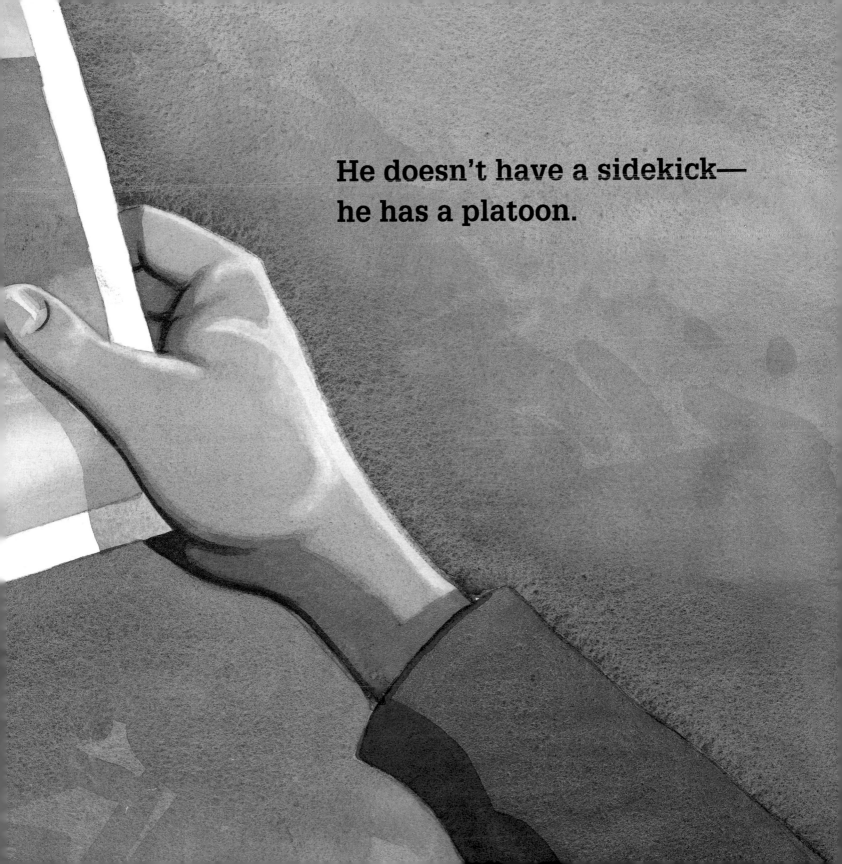

He doesn't have a sidekick—
he has a platoon.

Sometimes he has to go away for long trips,
but that's what superheroes have to do.

My dad is an American soldier.

My dad is a hero,
my superhero.